PLANETARY
EXPLORATION

MARS

SIMONE PAYMENT

Britannica®
Educational Publishing

IN ASSOCIATION WITH

ROSEN
EDUCATIONAL SERVICES

Published in 2017 by Britannica Educational Publishing (a trademark of Encyclopædia Britannica, Inc.) in association with The Rosen Publishing Group, Inc.
29 East 21st Street, New York, NY 10010

Distributed exclusively by Rosen Publishing.
To see additional Britannica Educational Publishing titles, go to rosenpublishing.com.

First Edition

Britannica Educational Publishing
J.E. Luebering: Executive Director, Core Editorial
Mary Rose McCudden: Editor, Britannica Student Encyclopedia

Rosen Publishing
Nicholas Croce: Editor
Nelson Sá: Art Director
Michael Moy: Designer
Cindy Reiman: Photography Manager
Karen Huang: Photo Researcher

Library of Congress Cataloging-in-Publication Data

Names: Payment, Simone.
Title: Mars / Simone Payment.
Description: New York : Britannica Educational Publishing in association with Rosen Educational Services, 2017. | Series: Planetary exploration | Includes bibliographical references and index.
Identifiers: LCCN 2016020475 | ISBN 9781508104131 (library bound) | ISBN 9781508104148 (pbk.) | ISBN 9781508103066 (6-pack)
Subjects: LCSH: Mars (Planet)—Juvenile literature. | Solar system—Juvenile literature.
Classification: LCC QB641 .P39 2017 | DDC 523.43—dc23
LC record available at https://lccn.loc.gov/2016020475

Manufactured in China

CONTENTS

MEET MARS, THE RED PLANET

Mars is one of the planets that orbit, or travel around, the sun in the **solar system**. It is the fourth planet from the sun. It is also Earth's outer neighbor. Mars is close enough that we can see it from Earth without using a telescope.

Mars is called "the red planet" because its surface is red. Sometimes it even looks like a red star in the night sky from Earth.

In this photograph of Mars, the white areas are clouds surrounding volcanoes.

Mars is about 142 million miles (228 million kilometers) away from the sun. It has two small, rocky moons called Phobos and Deimos.

For centuries, people have wondered whether there is life on Mars. So far, scientists have found no obvious signs of life on the planet. However, they are still trying to find out if life forms may have ever existed on Mars. Scientists are also studying whether there was ever water on Mars.

Earth

moon

From Mars, Earth and our moon look like stars. This photo was taken from Mars in 2014.

HOW BIG IS MARS?

Mars is the second smallest planet in the solar system. Mercury is the only planet that is smaller. The diameter of Mars, or the distance through its center, is about 4,224 miles (6,800 kilometers). That is about half the size of Earth's diameter.

This illustration shows the relative sizes of the planets in our solar system. Earth is the third from the the sun (left). Mars is the fourth.

Mars is smaller than Earth. But Earth and Mars have about the same amount of dry land. How can that be?

Mars is tiny if you compare it to the largest planet in the solar system, which is Jupiter. Jupiter has a diameter of about 89,000 miles (143,000 kilometers). That is about twenty-one times larger than Mars. In fact, Jupiter is two and a half times larger than all the other planets in the solar system put together.

The storm on Jupiter known as the Great Red Spot (center right) is 10,250 miles (16,496 kilometers) across, or more than twice the diameter of Mars.

INSIDE OF MARS

Like Earth, Mars has layers. Scientists think that Mars' center is a metal core that is mostly made of iron. Around the core is the mantle. The mantle is likely very thick. Scientists think that it is not completely hard but it is not completely melted either. It is like a rocky paste.

Unlike Earth, Mars does not have tectonic plates in its crust. Because of this, Mars' surface does not move about. Over time, as volcanoes erupt, the lava that pours out and hardens adds new layers of rock. This is why the volcanoes

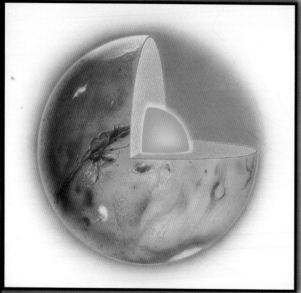

This illustration shows what scientists think the inside of Mars may look like, with a metal core at the center.

Scientists think that active volcanoes may still exist on Mars. What kinds of activity might you expect to occur in Mars' mantle to cause a volcanic eruption on Mars' surface?

on Mars are large compared to those on Earth.

Mars has the largest volcano on any planet in the solar system. It is called Olympus Mons. It is 16 miles (24 kilometers) tall. That is about three times higher than the tallest mountain on Earth, Mount Everest. Olympus Mons is also very wide. It is about the size of the state of Arizona.

This is a drawing of Olympus Mons. Scientists are not sure if it could erupt again someday.

The surface of Mars is made of rock and dust. Most of the rock and dust are a reddish brown color. This is because there is a lot of a substance called iron oxide in the rock. On Earth, rust is a well-known form of iron oxide that can be reddish in color.

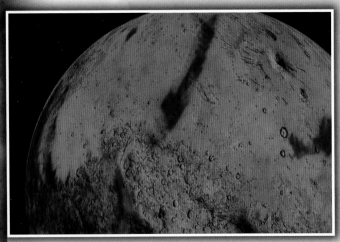

There are many large dust storms on Mars. Parts of the planet have many craters. There are also plains, deep valleys, and high mountains.

Mars' **atmosphere** contains a little oxygen but

Mars is reddish in color because its soil contains iron oxide.

The atmosphere is the layer of gases that surrounds a planet. The gases are held close to a planet by a force called gravity.

not enough for humans to be able to breathe. The atmosphere is mostly carbon dioxide and small amounts of other gases.

It is very cold on Mars. It is usually about −82 degrees F (−63 degrees C). In winter near its poles, it can get as cold as −195 degrees F (−125 degrees C). However, at noon in summer near the equator it can be about 70 degrees F (20 C).

This image shows the layer of gases above the surface of Mars.

THE MOONS OF MARS

Mars has two moons, called Phobos and Deimos. Unlike Earth's moon, Phobos and Deimos are not round. They are shaped a little like potatoes.

Phobos is the larger moon. It is about 16.5 miles (27 kilometers) long and 13 miles (21 kilometers) across. Deimos is just 9.5 miles (15 kilometers) around.

It does not take Phobos and Deimos long to orbit

Someday Phobos may break apart because of the strong pressure from Mars' gravity.

around Mars. Phobos is closer to Mars. It takes only about 8 hours for it to orbit Mars. Deimos orbits Mars in a little more than 30 hours.

Some scientists believe that Phobos and Deimos are **asteroids**. They think the moons were floating in space and began orbiting Mars when they were captured by Mars' gravity.

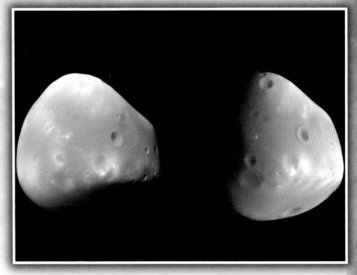

The moons Deimos and Phobos were named after the sons of Ares, the ancient Greek god of war. In ancient Rome, Ares was known as Mars.

A LARGE ORBIT

Like all planets, Mars has two types of motion: orbit and spin. Mars orbits, or travels around, the sun. It completes one orbit every 687 Earth days. In other words, a year on Mars lasts 687 Earth days. This makes a Mars year almost two times as long as an Earth year.

Like all planets, Mars' path around the sun is oval-shaped. Mars has a longer oval-shaped orbit than Earth does. This means that

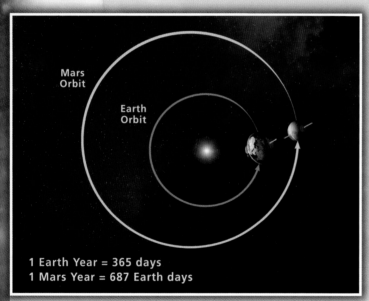

Mars Orbit

Earth Orbit

1 Earth Year = 365 days
1 Mars Year = 687 Earth days

Mars completes one orbit every 687 Earth days, which is almost two Earth years.

Gravity is a force that pulls between all objects. Objects with more mass have more gravity. How do you think Mars' gravity compares with the sun's gravity?

Mars is sometimes much farther away from the sun than it is at other times. When it is farthest from the sun, it is 155 million miles (249 million kilometers) away. When it is closest, it is about 128 million miles (207 million kilometers) away.

As Mars orbits the sun, Mars' moons orbit the planet.

MARS' SPIN

Mars spins on its axis at nearly the same speed as Earth does. An axis is an imaginary line that goes through the center of a planet. Mars takes about 24.6 hours to complete one rotation. So a Mars day, called a "sol," lasts just a little longer than a day on Earth.

Mars' axis is tilted a little bit in relation to the sun. This makes Mars have seasons. During parts of Mars' orbit one

The sun looks smaller in Mars' sky than it does in Earth's sky because Mars is farther away from the sun than Earth is.

half of the planet gets more sunlight than the other. The halves of the planet are called hemispheres.

As Mars' winter season approaches in the northern hemisphere, an ice cap forms at the north pole. This is because that half of the planet is tilted away from the sun. The northern ice cap starts to melt as summer approaches. Mars' southern hemisphere experiences winter when its northern hemisphere experiences summer.

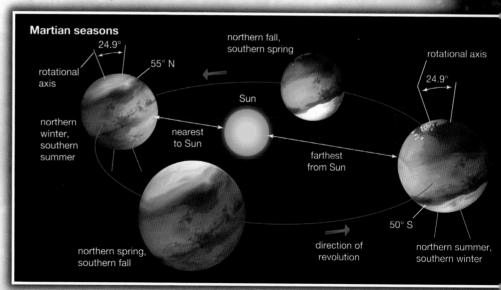

Martian seasons

24.9°

rotational axis

55° N

northern fall, southern spring

rotational axis

24.9°

northern winter, southern summer

nearest to Sun

Sun

farthest from Sun

northern spring, southern fall

direction of revolution

50° S

northern summer, southern winter

This image illustrates the Martian seasons. The seasons change depending how the planet is tilted toward or away from the sun.

ANCIENT OBSERVATION

People have been observing Mars since ancient times. Before telescopes were invented, people could only study Mars with the naked eye. They were able to tell Mars was a planet because it moved across the sky. Ancient people noticed that Mars was reddish in color. The color reminded them of blood. Some named the planet after their god of death. Others

This ancient Roman coin bears the image of the mythological figure Mars, the god of war.

Ancient astronomers noticed that, over time, some objects moved across the sky and other objects did not. How would this observation help them understand that some objects were stars and some were planets?

named the planet after their god of war. Mars is the name of the Roman god of war.

Astronomers were able to see Mars much more clearly after telescopes were invented. Some astronomers thought they were seeing canals on the surface. They thought maybe there were rivers on Mars or even that Martians had made the canals.

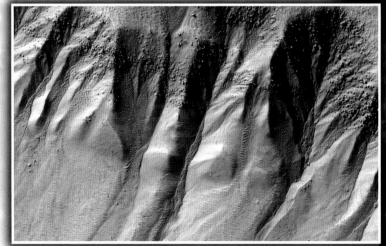

These gullies on Mars show rocks and boulders that have rolled downhill after frost has melted.

THE MARINER MISSIONS

S ince 1964 many unmanned spacecraft have been sent to explore Mars. Some were designed to fly by or to orbit Mars. Other unmanned space-craft landed on the surface of the planet.

The United States' National **Aeronautics** and Space Administration (NASA) sent several Mariner spacecraft to Mars. Mariner 4, Mariner 6, and Mariner 7 took photos as they flew by the planet.

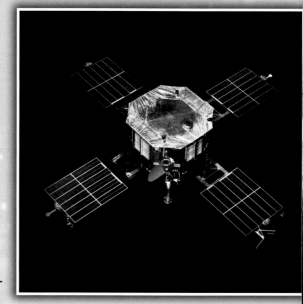

This is a photograph of one of NASA's Mariner spacecraft.

Aeronautics is the science of flight and operation of aircraft.

In 1971, NASA's Mariner 9 became the first spacecraft to orbit Mars. It took pictures of the surface of Mars. The pictures showed canyons and volcanoes. They also showed what looked like empty riverbeds. This made people wonder if there had once been water on Mars.

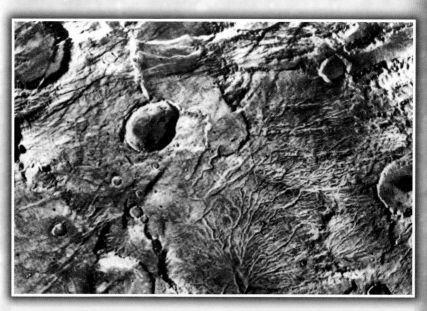

Mariner 9 took this photo of Mars' surface in 1972 as it orbited Mars.

FIRST VISITS

In 1976, NASA's Viking 1 and Viking 2 spacecraft landed successfully on Mars.

Each Viking spacecraft had an orbiter and a lander. When they reached Mars, the orbiter took pictures of Mars from space. The landers went to the surface.

The landers took photos on the surface and tested the atmosphere and soil. The Viking landers were looking for any signs of life. However, they did not find any evidence that there is life on Mars.

The Viking 1 lander took this photo of Mars' surface in 1976. Parts of the lander can be seen in the picture.

THINK ABOUT IT

Early missions to Mars were mostly focused on finding water. What discoveries might help scientists figure out if water is present on Mars?

The United States and Europe have sent several spacecraft to orbit the planet since the 1990s. These spacecraft included the Mars Global Surveyor and the Mars Odyssey from the United States and the Mars Express from Europe. They took many pictures of the surface of Mars. It appears in some pictures that water may flow on Mars at certain times of year.

The Mars Global Surveyor took this photo of the sides of a crater during winter on Mars.

"ROVING" AROUND

The US spacecraft Pathfinder landed on Mars in 1997. It released a robot, or rover, called Sojourner on the surface. Sojourner took photographs and gathered samples of the soil. The rover performed many tests of the samples to check for signs of water and life.

The United States later sent two more rovers, called Spirit and Opportunity. They landed on Mars in 2004. Each rover landed at a different location. Each was equipped with several

The Sojourner rover took more than 500 pictures and did many experiments on the surface of Mars.

COMPARE AND CONTRAST

The Spirit and Opportunity rovers were tested for years on Earth before they were sent to Mars. Which regions on Earth might be good testing grounds for the rovers?

cameras and instruments to find out what Mars' surface is made of and to check for signs of water. Spirit and Opportunity found clues that there may have been a large body of salty water on Mars many years ago.

The rovers explored Mars for several years. Their missions lasted much longer than scientists expected on the rocky, cold, dusty surface of the planet.

The Curiosity rover took this selfie with its robotic arm.

PHOENIX, CURIOSITY, AND MAVEN

Phoenix was the third rover mission to Mars. It landed in 2008 and used its robotic arm to dig a ditch in the Martian soil. Phoenix found ice below the surface. This was more evidence of water on Mars.

In 2012 a fourth rover, called Curiosity, landed on Mars. Curiosity is the biggest, heaviest rover ever sent to Mars. It has studied many samples of the soil.

MAVEN has discovered that energy from the sun (solar wind) may have changed the climate on Mars millions of years ago.

Instead of looking for water, the goal of the Curiosity was to see if Mars was, or is, able to support life. What other things besides water do you think the Curiosity looked for?

The Mars Atmosphere and Volatile EvolutioN (MA-VEN) spacecraft has been orbiting Mars since 2014. It collects information about the planet's atmosphere. Scientists hope this information will show them how Mars' atmosphere has changed over time. This may give them clues about whether there was once life on the planet.

This photo taken by Phoenix shows frost on the surface. The frost melted when the sun rose several hours later.

INTO THE FUTURE

NASA and other space agencies around the world are planning more missions to Mars. NASA's InSight mission will explore the inside of the planet. The European Space Agency is planning missions that will look for more signs of past life on Mars.

NASA is designing a new Mars rover that is scheduled to launch in 2020. This rover will look for evidence that life can exist on Mars. This evi-

The heat shield and shell of the InSight spacecraft protect the lander from heat and pressure from the atmosphere of Mars.

THINK ABOUT IT

In 2020, Mars and Earth will be as close as possible to each other. How might this be helpful for the launch of the Mars rover in 2020?

dence would help NASA determine if humans could go to Mars.

For thousands of years people have looked into the night sky and dreamed of visiting Mars. Could this dream come true someday?

Scientists continue to search for evidence of water on Mars. They think that this image shows that rivers once flowed on the planet.

ASTRONOMER A scientist who studies all of the objects outside of Earth's atmosphere.

ATMOSPHERE A mass of gases surrounding a body in outer space.

CANAL An artificial waterway for boats or for draining or irrigating land.

CANYON A deep narrow valley with steep sides.

CARBON DIOXIDE An odorless, colorless gas that is naturally present in air.

COMET A small chunk of dust and ice that orbits the sun.

CORE The central part of a planet.

CRATER A hole made by an impact (as in a meteorite).

DIAMETER The measurement of a straight line passing through the center of a figure or body, especially a sphere or circle.

DITCH A long narrow channel or trench.

ERUPT To burst forth or explode.

EVIDENCE Information that tells if something is true.

IRON A heavy, magnetic, silver-white metallic element.

LANDER A type of spacecraft that lands on the surface of a planet or moon.

MANTLE The middle layer of a planet between the crust (surface) and the core (center portion).

ORBITER A type of spacecraft that flies around a planet in order to study the planet.

PLAIN A broad area of level or rolling treeless country.

ROTATION One complete turn around an axis or center.

ROVER A robotic spacecraft that lands on the surface of a planet or moon and then moves around to explore or perform tests.

SPACECRAFT A vehicle for travel and exploration beyond Earth's atmosphere.

TELESCOPE A device that uses lenses, or curved mirrors and lenses, to make distant objects look closer and larger.

FOR MORE INFORMATION

Books

Graham, Ian. *Planets Near Earth*. Mankato, MN: Smart Apple Media, 2015.

Lawrence, Ellen. *Mars: The Dusty Planet*. Cornwall, UK: Ruby Tuesday Books, 2014.

Lomberg, Michelle. *Mars*. New York, NY: Weigl, 2014.

Oxlade, Chris. *Mars*. Chicago, IL: Raintree, 2013.

Reilly, Carmel. *The Planets*. New York, NY: Marshall Cavendish, 2012.

Websites

Because of the changing nature of internet links, Rosen Publishing has developed an online list of websites related to the subject of this book. This site is updated regularly. Please use this link to access this list:

http://www.rosenlinks.com/PE/mars

INDEX